RICK

"THE REAPER"

The first time I laid eyes on her, I knew she was mine. The missing piece of my soul. The girl of my dreams.

I couldn't stop obsessing over her. All those nights I spent in my lonely bed, fixated on her photos until I spilled onto them. Her smooth thighs and full bosom. Her pursed lips and crooked smile. I wanted her. Not in a nice little "feed her ice cream" sort of way. Something messed up. Something bad.

Oh, the things I would do... Some would make her bleed. Some would never heal.

She was mine by birthright, and I had to claim her.

Five of Him
A Dark Romantic Thriller

Katrina Yang

CONTENTS

JAMES
"THE PROTECTOR"

We've been down this road before. Jumping to conclusions before the process is complete. The search for the perfect woman requires time, patience, research, and proof.

A boner is just what it is, a reaction of a young body to arousal. I once got hard from staring at a hole in a tree, and the tree certainly isn't the woman of my dreams. A hard-on is not proof. *That's simply ridiculous.*

I sigh and slam my money on the counter, disturbed by the thoughts running through my mind these days.

"One room, please." I nod at the clerk.

My eyes wander down the hallway of this old, stinky motel at the edge of town. It looks even worse than I remember. Out of five lamps in the hallway, only two are working this time, and yet I'm paying for a room, just like the other eighteen guests staying here tonight.

There's a certain group of people who choose where

they stay based on location, anonymity, and discretion, and I'm one of them. Motel 808 offers all of the above. It's right across the street from the Denny's where the girl works, and I'm here to watch her.

"Same room?" the clerk asks.

"How about 207? Better view."

"It's not available."

"307?"

"Sorry."

"What about 205, 209, 305, 309? You gotta have one for me."

"No... They're all booked."

"Seriously?"

He looks at me impatiently.

"Same room it is then." I raise my brows, slightly disappointed. "107. My lucky number."

107 has the clearest view of the girl, but it only works when traffic is light. 105 and 109 are both acceptable alternatives. Then again, none of them match what the second floor can offer.

Maybe next time. I grab the room keys and put my things in the room. Then I cross the street.

She's working tonight.

The doorbell rings as I push the door open, and there I am, standing in her presence. She turns to look at me from the soda fountain, and for a brief moment, our eyes meet across the diner.

Daisy Maxwell.

I know everything there is to know about her: where she lives, when her shift starts and ends, who her best friend is, and whether she's dating anyone. Her favorite flavor of ice cream is vanilla. She listens to Eminem and has an annoyingly sweet habit of making fruit muffins on rainy days.

I ask for a window seat facing the soda fountain and grab a salt packet to rub between my fingers. Just a little something to distract me from the increasing discomfort of my arousal pressing against my pants. I watch her carry three cups of Coke to the table behind me.

She wipes her hand on her apron and heads my way. I quickly lower my head, my fingers rubbing the salt packet a little faster.

"Hey, you look familiar," she says in a bright voice. "Have I seen you before?"

I look up. My gaze falls on her lips, noticing the curve at the corner of her mouth. She's put on some lip gloss, sparkly and in a shade of pink I like.

"Yeah, I've been here a few times," I murmur. "It's my favorite diner."

Her eyes linger on my face a moment longer, then she lowers them, as if my gaze is too intense.

"What brings you to town?" she asks after clearing her throat. "Do you know anyone here?"

"You." I can't help but draw a smile at the idea of her,

my eyes lowering to the name tag on her chest. "I like to look at pretty girls with flower names."

"You're too sweet," she says, and I watch her smile widen. A dimple forms in her cheek.

"Not as sweet as your fruit muffins." I swallow. "It was rainy this morning. Am I right?"

"You know about my rainy day muffins?" She widens her eyes. "You must have been here a lot."

"Oh, you have no idea." I toss the salt packet on the table, leaning back. "Glad to finally be noticed."

She clicks the back of her pen several times, as if nervous.

"I'm Daisy," she says.

"James Bell."

I've sat in this exact booth ten times this year, observing her, taking pictures of her. Eight out of those ten times, she was too busy to pay me any attention—breakups, new flings, girl fights. She kept herself busy, which made it easy for me to stay off her radar.

Over time, I've grown bolder, more reckless. Which led to this unfortunate exchange.

"What's your last name, sweetheart?" I ask, unable to help myself.

She bites her lip slightly, as if the question is a bit intrusive, so I explain.

"A beautiful woman like yourself deserves more respect than a flowery name." I shift in my seat. "I know three Daisies in my life. You sure don't look like any of them, and believe me, I mean it as a compliment."

She clicks the pen again, rocking back and forth. She does this whenever she feels flutters in her stomach. I know this because I've seen it before—with the busboys she had a thing for, and then her boss. It seems that today, I'm the one.

My fingers reach for the salt packet again.

"Daisy Maxwell," she says shyly.

"Daisy Maxwell," I repeat in a whisper. "You remind me of someone I know."

Her pupils dilate slightly.

"My late wife," I explain. "Especially when you smile."

And there it is—that look of shock on her face as she realizes I've been married.

"I'm sorry..." She bites her lower lip, as if unsure what to say next. "I wouldn't have guessed it. I mean, you look so young."

"A man can be widowed at any age," I say, looking her in the eye. "But I'll take that as a compliment."

She bites her lip again. I've made her nervous again, and for some reason, I like it.

"So, um, what brought you to town?" she asks. "You didn't answer me before."

"A woman," I say without flinching.

Her smile freezes, and I catch a hint of disappointment on her face. I rub the salt packet a bit faster, recognizing her attachment to me. She has a tendency to become too emotionally involved with the ones she likes —perhaps a little too fast at times.

"Don't worry, sweetheart. I'm just doing a friend a favor, checking on his girl."

"Oh..." She seems a little relieved. Her fingers seek the pen again. She clicks the back of it. "How long are you staying?"

"The plan is to leave first thing in the morning," I say softly, my eyes locked on her face. "I could stay a bit."

She nods thoughtfully, though she can't hide the disappointment on her face.

"You grew up in this town?" I ask.

"Yeah..."

"How do you like it here?"

"It's... fine."

"That doesn't sound like fine to me."

"I do like it here..." she blurts. "It's just a really small town, and sometimes a place like this can mess with your head, you know?"

"Like you're trapped in a place too small to hold all parts of you."

"Yeah, like that." She nods.

My eyes drift back to the menu. My fingers glide across the plastic surface.

"Do you travel a lot?" she asks. "You have this... vibe. Like you've seen things."

I raise a brow, not entirely sure what she means, but my lips move anyway.

"I have."

"I'd like to hear about them sometime," she says shyly, her fingernails digging into the side of the pen.

"How about tonight?" The words jump out of my mouth before I can stop them. My heart races. "I'd like to learn a few more things about you as well."

"I'd love that," she whispers. "But my shift doesn't end until eleven."

"You got a date afterward?"

"No." She shakes her head.

"Then I'll wait," I say, pointing at the motel across the street. "You know 808?"

"Yeah."

"I have a room there, but I'm not in a rush to go back all by myself."

"It's certainly not the best spot in town," she says, as if she knows something about the place. I sense she wants to tell me more, but she presses her lips together and lowers her voice. "There are rumors, you know. I mean, if you'd like to stay somewhere else, I can recommend a place or two."

"Anywhere you like," I say with a smile.

"So... tonight, after my shift."

"Yeah."

"Okay then."

She takes out her notepad at last, smiling as if she's been holding it hostage the whole time.

"What would you like, James?"

RICK

"THE REAPER"

My fingers curl into a fist, heat coiling low in my body. There are rules. Lines we don't cross. Protocol. Research is just supposed to be what it is: observation, background checks, and light stalking. No interaction. No getting himself a date with my girl.

That first conversation was supposed to be mine. She was supposed to feel all the flutters in her stomach with me.

I flex my chin, rolling my neck until it cracks.

"Hi, Daisy," I call the little waitress over, trying not to lose my cool. "Can you remind me what I've ordered?"

"Coke, steak dinner, a side of fries, and a cheesecake," she recites. "Did I get it right?"

"What a good girl." I try to keep my voice soft, but something rough slips through anyway. "I've changed my mind about the steak dinner. I'll have the nachos. Extra jalapeños and cream."

"Mmm spicy."

"You like that too, don't you?"

She looks at me, and whatever she sees in my eyes makes her press her lips together and swallow.

"Sweet girl, give me a beer and vanilla ice cream in a cone."

"You like vanilla ice cream, too?"

"It's my favorite."

"Then we should share."

She hesitates. She goes still under my gaze for a moment. By the time she snaps out of it, she looks flushed and startled. She presses that notepad back into her pocket and hurries away.

A little while later, she circles back.

"We can share one after my shift," she says, keeping her eyes on the table as her fingers brush my arm.

"You sure we can wait?"

I make no effort to hide how hard I am.

She walks away, but she looks back at me a few times. One of those times, I lick my lips and lock her gaze in mine, not letting her look away until her breath turns uneven. She blinks, trying to pull herself together.

I keep doing it every time she steals a glance at me, until she simply can't anymore.

"Excuse me," she mutters, heading to the back.

I push my fists harder against the table and stand up. In other times, I'd flirt with her a bit more over the next couple of hours, until the taste of desire becomes desperate, and this little dance between us turns inevitable. But

James crossed a line today. He made her like him. He made her want him. Him. Not me. And that's unacceptable.

I follow her to the back. There, against the wall, I find her with a cigarette. I walk up to her, take the disgusting thing from her hand, and throw it into the dumpster.

She slides a little down the wall as I lock her between my arms. Our bodies touch. She looks like she's still debating what's going to happen, but her hand already reaches for mine, guiding me under her apron.

"James..." she whispers. A soft moan slips out. Her eyes look hopelessly into mine, like a silent plea telling me she shouldn't be doing this, while her hand presses me harder between her legs.

I press my thumb to her soft lips, pulling them apart.

"Call me Rick," I correct her.

"Rick."

"That's it," I whisper, feeling her melt under me. "That's my girl."

I lick her upper lip as I push my thumb past her teeth. I bite her lower lip, sucking it as she reaches for my belt. Her small hand strokes me over my pants.

"How long have you known?"

"Since you called me to change your order."

"That's the right answer."

I turn her around and peel off her panties.

"You got a condom?" she barely manages to get out.

"Yes."

I take one out and put it on, then pin her hands behind her back, like my little prisoner.

"Say my name again."

"Rick."

"Again."

"Rick..."

What comes next is her muffled cry against my palm as I slam hard into her. She takes the whole thing in and squeezes me tight, wet and needy, as if she's been waiting for this the whole time.

"Horny girl." I pull her closer to me. "Your shift isn't even over yet, and here you are, being fucked into a wall."

I lift her a little and bend her over.

"Tell me, do you do this often?"

She shakes her head.

"How many times?"

She shakes her head again, unable to talk with my hand over her mouth.

"Good girl." I grip her ponytail, picking up the pace.

"Good. Girl."

I bounce her hard on my cock, letting the sound of us fucking fill the alley. She makes sweet noises where our bodies meet, messy and desperate.

"I want to take off that condom and fuck all my swimmers into you." I pull her hair to the side and whisper into her ear.

She pulses around me suddenly.

"What do you say? We keep fucking like it's a sport. I

make you come, and we go back into the diner. Or—you let me cream you up."

She swings her hips wilder at my words. Her pussy tightens, then releases, tempted and wanting. I know she can't resist it. She's my girl. She wants everything reckless and hot, just like me.

I give her a couple hard thrusts. My hands cup her ass and part her cheeks, readying her.

"Take it off," she begs at last. "I want you to take the condom off, and—"

"Fuck my swimmers into you," I finish for her and pull my cock out. I rip the condom off, then push back inside, hot and naked. A heavier sound pulls up from deep inside her as if she feels the difference.

"That's my girl." I pull her even closer to me. My fingers press into her mouth as I hold her, mounting her from behind.

I don't remember everything that happened after that. Just the intensity of it—hot, messed up, and a little violent.

I give her all I have. All at once. Everything I've dreamed of doing to her.

She cries so loudly that even a hand over her mouth can't keep her down. She keeps making those wild noises until her belly is full. Then she goes still, looking so pretty with her shoulders covered in my marks and blood, her ass swollen and red.

"Wow…" she mutters, still catching her breath. "That was—"

"Too much?" I ask, wiping the tear from the corner of her eye. My eyes fall on her bruised lips.

"No." She swallows, shaking her head rapidly. "You kidding me?"

"Tell me." I rub my thumb over her lower lip, the dried blood crumbling on my skin.

My heart still races, but I feel my lips curve.

"Is it too soon to say I love you?" she jokes.

"Yes." I pull up her panties for her, then press a kiss to her forehead as I redo my belt. "You're a crazy girl, Daisy."

I'm a little surprised that she liked it. My intensity has always been more of a curse, and because of that, I've never been able to be with the same woman twice.

The girl of my dreams. My missing puzzle piece. She's mine, and I'll never let go.

"Fuck... I, um... I should get back. I'm not really supposed to be out here."

"Not supposed to fuck a customer either," I tease.

She flattens her apron and smooths her hair, trying to pretend she's still the same girl. I let her do what she has to do, but no matter what she does, she can't hide those marks. I made sure they'd be seen.

"Don't forget our date."

She tries to slip away without a kiss, so I grab her and pull her back to me, pressing a kiss to her lips. It tastes like blood, mine and hers.

"You still want to?"

"A date is a date," I whisper, looking her in the eye.

"Just because I've had a taste doesn't mean I don't want more. I still want to fatten you up and learn a few things about you. Later tonight, I'll take you to my motel room and do what we just did again."

"You're trouble, Rick." She bites her lip.

"You have no idea."

I plant my hand on her sweet ass and kiss her again before she leaves. I watch her disappear through the door.

I will take her again later in the night. Then again in the morning. Then again during her shift. Then again and again until she misses her period, until she carries a part of me inside.

ME
"THE IDIOT"

I open my eyes and find myself standing in front of a mirror. I look... skinnier than I remember. My hair has grown long. I'm wearing a flannel shirt, baggy jeans, and boots. My keys hang from a belt loop. I look like I haven't slept for days, but that's not what's alarming. What's alarming is the thick iron taste in my mouth and this coconut smell on my hands—like a woman's shampoo, body cream, or something.

Sweat clings to my skin under my shirt. My muscles feel oddly relaxed, like I've been doing something physical.

What the fuck did I do this time? My heart starts to race. There's an unnerving, suffocating dread pulsing through my nerves, hinting at something terrible.

I turn on the faucet and splash water on my face. When I look up at myself again, I notice a cut on my upper lip and scratches around my neck. I tug down my shirt and find more marks across my shoulders.

My fingernails are dirty, like I've been digging in the dirt.

Shit... Not this again. I look around and notice I'm in a public bathroom. I move to lock the door, only to realize it's already locked.

Shit. I shove my hands under the water, add soap, and scrub hard. I dig under my nails until angry redness blooms.

It's blood, for fuck's sake.

And what's with the discomfort in my jeans? My junk feels wet and a little sticky. I unbuckle my belt and pull it free. I bring my fingers to my nose.

No, no, no! I get more soap and scrub even harder, scraping the blood from beneath my nails, trying to erase her scent—her blood, her DNA, all proof of me with her.

I twist my arm to check the scratches again. They look fresh, like whatever happened took place minutes ago.

The world goes quiet for a moment as a loud ringing fills my ears. A throbbing headache slams into my temple like a sledgehammer.

Bang. I clench my teeth, fighting the spin.

The next thing I know, I'm outside the bathroom, walking past a kitchen.

Wait—am I at a Denny's?

Then I see her. No. More like I recognize her—the waitress with beautiful green eyes and hickeys peeking out from her uniform. I've never met her in my life, and yet I have this unsettling feeling that something happened between us.

"The nachos are ready. I put them on your table already. So is the beer you asked for," she murmurs to me as she walks by, her fingers brushing against my arm.

She's not dead! I let out a breath of relief. No. She's very much alive.

My heart slows. The edge of my lips lifts into a curve. My legs move on their own, following her to my table.

I sit down and start stuffing my mouth with nachos. I don't remember the last time I ate. It must have been a long time ago—long before Rick and his messed-up spree. I'm fully enjoying the food when something dreadful quietly clicks into place.

I freeze, my heart pounding louder and louder as I start to understand what's happening. This thing— whatever this is between Rick and her—is still going on. I didn't wake up in the aftermath this time.

Shit. I have to warn her. I need to warn her before it's too late.

"Daisy—"

RICK

"THE REAPER"

I shove the idiot back into the mental cage where he belongs before he ruins the perfect night.

"Daisy, darling." I soften my smile and gesture for the sweet girl to come closer. The way her legs rub together, a little awkwardly, tells me she's still feeling the aftereffects of what we did in that alley.

"Rick." She stops by the table, her fingers curling to touch my arm.

"How about we eat that ice cream now?" I say in a low voice, catching her hand and pressing a kiss to it.

A moment later, she comes back with a vanilla ice cream cone topped with a cherry.

I grab the cherry by the stem. Her eyes glisten, so I twist it between my fingers and gesture for her to come closer. She takes the fruit between her lips; her tongue tugs against it.

I watch her swallow. The little dip at her throat

bounces back. My breath grows heavier. I start to feel the strain in my pants again, thinking about the things we'll do together later tonight.

"Take your time, baby," I whisper. "This is all I'm getting until your shift ends."

The idiot in my head goes quiet, just like before. He turns his back on us, unable to handle the intensity of our desires.

For the rest of the night, I let my girl work. She reroutes her path to pass my table now and then, and every time my nose picks up the familiar scent of her coconut shampoo, she brushes her fingers against my arm, letting me know it's her. So I keep ordering soft drinks, then more French fries, to keep her close.

We skip the date at the end of her shift and head straight back to my motel room across the street. I press her onto the bed, take my belt off, and tie her hands to the headboard.

"I think I just discovered that I might have a breeding kink," she says, swallowing hard as her panties come off.

"That's my girl." I grin.

I break her out of her dress while she takes me like the good girl she is. My hand roams over her chest, then settles on her lower belly.

"I'm going to fill you up again," I declare.

She nods, eagerly.

"Say my name," I demand.

"You have to earn it," she whispers, pressing her lips to my earlobe, moaning hard. So, I make her wait, letting her work up and down my cock under me on her own, my fingers sliding into her pussy, pressing against her sweet spot.

For hours, I edge her, making her all sweaty and weak, her lips tied tight. I refuse to give it to her even when she's crying my name and begging for release. I start fucking her harder and rougher, her toes curling, her voice going hoarse.

"Rick!" she shouts as I push out my load, her body tensing, trembling, her pussy gripping around me so tightly it locks every drop inside.

I grab a handful of her hair, closing my eyes, picturing my belt around her neck.

Because she's Daisy, and she wants me. Not soft. Not kind. Me. The whole fucking deal—the one who pulls a belt over her neck and makes her scream like bloody murder, the one who hears voices in his head and loses control.

That night, I pin her under me and unleash every single fantasy we have. I black out a few times, not sure what happens then. By the time she snuggles into my arms, clutching the belt, she's covered in marks—some I remember leaving, some I don't. Her butt cheeks are bruised. Blood smears across her legs.

I lower my gaze to the stinging pain in my arms, and that's when I see her name carved into my wrist.

There's a hair in my mouth. I spit it out, pinching it between my fingers. I lift it to my face and look at it closely, then get out of bed and head into the bathroom.

Time to clean myself up. After all that hard work, I'm pretty stinky.

I get in the shower and turn on the faucet. A familiar anxious feeling rises along my spine, and instead of fighting it, I just close my eyes and let it happen.

JAMES
"THE PROTECTOR"

Barbaric!

My lungs seize at the sight of red water spiraling down the drain. I stumble, squeezing my hands into fists. My body starts to shake, and everything goes thin and distant.

She was perfect. She was Daisy.

I did this to her.

I spotted her. I spent a year watching her, learning about her. I asked her on a date. I led him right to her—and the way that bastard treated her—

I twist the faucet to make the water hotter, trying not to think about how bad she looks. Rick did a real number on her. No care. No banter. Not even a decent meal. He just brought her back to this dingy motel and did whatever he wanted to her.

Pain chews through me like a chainsaw.

I knew. I knew what he was up to and what he's

capable of, and I did nothing to stop him. I did what I always do when it gets unbearable. I turned it off.

And now, she's gone.

I turn the faucet off and step out. I dry myself, then put the toilet lid down and sit on it instead of going back to that room. I'm a coward. I don't want to see her exposed, bruised, and hurt. Her hair scattered across the bedsheet.

I just can't do it.

I stand up, get dressed, and grab the keys. I open the door without looking at her and get into my truck. I pull out of the parking lot and hit the highway, determined to put as many miles as possible between me and that cursed town where my girl lived.

My shoulders shake at the thought of her sweet, crooked smile. I keep replaying our brief conversation from last night—harmless, lovely, normal. We could've gone on a date. We could've had something, if I weren't this... broken.

I pull over to the side of the road and slam my fist into the steering wheel. A broken sound claws its way out of my throat. I wish I were different. I wish I were someone else. Anyone. I wish my love meant protection and fun banter instead of destruction.

Take the helm from me. Anyone. Drive us back. 'Cause I can't.

The next time I open my eyes, I'm back in that motel, wearing the same shirt. My truck is parked outside. I'm sitting on the side of the bed with gum between my teeth. *Daisy.* I turn toward the bed, but my eyes squeeze shut at the sight of her.

Oh... It hurts to look at her. I have to do something. I can't not do something.

I get up and cross the street to the grocery store for medicine and Band-Aids. I come back, clean her wounds with antiseptic, and rub healing ointment into the bruises. I cover the scratches with bandages. It's pathetic, I know. Nothing can bring her back. But I just...

I pull a sock over her foot.

Her body moves.

I freeze.

"What are you doing, Rick?" she asks in a lazy voice, rubbing her eyes.

I shift my eyes to her tired face. She has dark bags under her eyes. Is she really talking to me? Or am I imagining her?

"Putting clothes on you," I murmur. My voice doesn't even sound like my own.

Her brows knit together.

"You're exposed..." I try to explain.

"I'm... fine," she mutters hesitantly. Her eyes fall on the bandages on her legs, and the knot between her brows grows. "Look, about last night."

"We don't have to talk about that."

Her eyes flicker. She freezes. Then, out of nowhere,

she shoots up in bed. Her face turns all red, and then white.

"I can't believe this," her voice trembling. "You're trying to cover me up."

"You were hurt..."

"Yeah!" She tears a Band-Aid off her arm. "That's the fucking point!"

"No... I..."

"Fuck you!" she shouts.

I want to explain to her it wasn't me, but my chest tightens when she starts peeling off the long trail of bandages on her leg.

"Daisy, I... you gotta understand..."

"No!" she shouts. "You need to listen to me! This is your guilt! Your shame! Yours. Not mine."

"What are you talking about?"

I feel so helpless. She's not making sense. This isn't making sense.

"Get out!" she screams. "Get the fuck out of my room!"

"Daisy..."

She hops off the bed and pushes me all the way to the door. She opens it and shoves my bag in my arms, then slams the door hard against my face.

I stare at the door, my arms hanging midair, my body hasn't caught up with what just happened—only that she opens the door again and drags me inside. She presses her lips against mine, biting my lip hard.

Everything in my arms falls on the ground at once, all

over the place. I pull her away from me, shocked and a little horrified.

"I earned those last night," she whispers, looking me in the eye, unbuttoning my shirt. "Don't... erase me."

No...

DEAN
"MAINTENANCE"

"You're right. I'm sorry."

I catch her busy hands trying to undress me and pin them behind her back. James crashed, again. So I'm back to clean up the mess. It must be nice to check out from time to time. Turn it off. Black out. Asshole doesn't even know I exist.

I lock the girl between my arms, press her head against my chest to calm my heart.

"I shouldn't have covered them up," I say, correcting James' mistake. "I woke up and saw you hurt. I panicked. I worried that I'd gone too far."

"You could never go too far with me," Daisy says in a muffled voice. "I liked it, Rick. I loved it. I've never had something this intense with anyone. And—" she swallows hard. "I'm sorry... I know you were just—"

"Stop talking..." I murmur, pressing her harder

against my chest to soothe the urges. It's not working. Not when she's saying those things.

"I... I get angry sometimes," she continues, her eyes a little red. "I lose control, and I... I ruin things."

"You didn't ruin anything." I close my eyes and cover her mouth, stopping her from saying another word—but she catches my hand and bites my index finger, her tongue wetting my skin. She pulls her arms free and clutches around me, and a soft moan slips from my lips.

Shit. A dangerous urge rises in me, sudden and overwhelming. I quickly pull my finger back and place my hands on each side of her face. I plant a kiss on her forehead as a compromise, but she steps on tiptoe and locks my lips before I can stop her.

The moment she touches me, my chest seizes. The room tilts. I grip her by the shoulders and pull her away, irritated by the pressure building inside me. I'm barely holding the balance. Her coming onto me is making the job much harder.

"The water pressure is good," I blurt out. "You can take a shower if you'd like."

"Sounds good," she whispers. She leans closer to me, her hand reaching back.

I didn't mean that. I swallow and catch her hand before anything happens.

"Daisy, you need time to heal," I beg.

"I need time with you," she moans, biting her lower lip. Her eyes tighten when her teeth accidentally touch the cut, but she ignores it.

"Are you leaving today?" she pants.

"That's the plan. Yes."

"Denver?"

"Yeah."

"What time do you have to leave?"

"Soon."

"Oh..." She tangles her fingers together.

I feel a small sting in my chest, not sure where it comes from.

"Take me again," she says, pulling away. "In the shower."

She jumps off the bed and slides behind the bathroom door, not giving me a chance to speak. The door closes—but not all the way. She leaves a slit open, just enough for me to see her in the shower.

I stay on the bed, frustrated and stuck. I have a feeling she's expecting me to follow her in there. But I can't join her. I won't. I roll my eyes, taking my eyes off the door gap.

This is ridiculous.

I straighten up, annoyed by the pressure in my pants. I can feel Rick sneaking in, feeding me those filthy images. My eyes flash back to her, naked in the shower. She catches me looking and reaches down, sliding a finger between her legs. I look away. Moans spill out of the shower as she touches herself. I let out a groan, feeling the discomfort intensify in my pants.

I shift on the bed, then something snaps inside me. I unzip my pants and take my cock out, my eyes drifting to her. I jerk off while she touches herself in the shower, her eyes locked on mine.

If this is how it goes, then let's get this over with. Once it's over, it's fucking over. At least that's what I thought.

The minute she comes out of the shower, needy and breathless, dripping wet with nothing but a towel wrapped around her, I just know I need to get out of here.

She glances at the wrinkled paper towels on the bed and unwraps the towel from herself.

"I'd like to take you somewhere," I say, a little breathless. "Is that okay?"

As soon as she nods, I grab the room keys and the rest of my things to check out. I wait for her in the truck until she comes out. She smells like motel soap and cheap shampoo and still stirs something deep inside me. I roll down the window and drive her to the pharmacy.

Her eyes dim when she realizes where I'm taking her, but this is necessary. I pull into the parking lot and unlock the doors. She follows me inside and watches me grab a few packs of Plan B pills from the shelf. The whole time, she's quiet.

"Don't let anyone sweet-talk you into having unprotected sex again," I say, looking at her. "Promise me."

"Yeah..." she mutters, avoiding my eyes.

"Including me." I sigh, my fingers tightening on the boxes.

I lead her to the line, but before it's our turn, she tugs on my sleeve. I turn to look at her, and there's something in her eyes—something that puzzles me. For a moment, I think she doesn't want the pills.

RICK

"THE REAPER"

Enough.

I drag her from the line to the shelf with the pills and shove the boxes back where they belong. Then I kiss her hard. A moan slips out as pain catches. She shoves her tongue in my mouth and deepens it, making the next sound from both of us filthy.

Boy, the way she melts underneath me, the way her hand strokes me over the fabric... she misses me. She's been missing me all morning. She should have me.

I take her hand and lead her to the bathroom. There, I press her against the wall and reach under her dress.

"You were gonna baby-trap me," I say in a hard whisper. "Still want to do just that?"

She bites her lip and nods, her hips pushing to my hand as she takes more of my fingers inside.

"Does it hurt?" I ask, trailing a kiss to her ear. My lips

fold her earlobe in. I suck on it, brushing her skin. "It's gonna hurt even more when I fuck you today."

She groans, her body trembling under my touch.

"I don't care," she breathes, working herself on my fingers. "Fuck me now, Rick."

"Good girl."

I take off my pants and press her to me. My tongue licks the sensitive spot behind her ear, touching the small bumps as she bites down on my shoulder and takes me.

The more I lick her there, the louder she is.

At first, I think it's just the sex. Then I start to wonder. Those bumps feel like marks. Scars. Healed. Old.

I pull her back and brush her hair away. My hand closes around her neck. Nausea rolls through me. I back away from her and drag my pants up. I recognize what it is, and the thought of saying her name makes me sick.

"Rick..." she tries. "Look, I—"

"Who is it?" I ask.

"What?"

"Give me a name."

"Rick, please..."

"No." I stop her before she says something I don't want to hear. "Give me a name. Or we're done."

I wipe my face and look around the bathroom. For the first time, I don't want to be here.

"Dylan," she murmurs at last, looking away.

Dylan Scofield. Yeah. I know who he is. He's the high school sweetheart.

DEAN

"MAINTENANCE"

I slip back in, taking the helm from Rick. He should've let me finish my job, and this could've been over ten minutes ago—but here we are.

"Let's go." I brush my fingers across her hairline and pull her hair over to cover the scar, then lead her back outside.

I grab a few boxes of pills from the shelf and get back in line. She looks at me from time to time, not sure what to say. I want to comfort her. I just don't think it's a good idea.

"There are things I can't take back..." she opens her mouth again.

I clench my teeth.

"You don't have to explain to me," I stop her. "Everyone has a past."

I pay for the pills and grab a few more packets of

condoms. I feel her hands tighten around my arms when I do, but she watches me and doesn't say a word.

In the car, I feed her the pills with some water, making sure she swallows them. Then I hand her the rest and the condoms.

"Take care of yourself, Daisy," I say in a soft voice. "Please."

She nods like she always does—unconvincingly.

"I guess this is it." She looks at me, a little hurt, as if I've punished her for something she's done in the past by making her take the pills.

"Yeah." I nod. "I'll see you later."

"Will you?"

She'll be surprised.

I curve my lips, knowing the things I can't say. I pull her in and plant a kiss on her forehead.

"See you, Daisy."

She lowers her eyes and opens the door. I watch her walk away. For some reason, my chest hurts.

I feel like I should've told her more, but it's not my job, and I'm running out of time. I start the truck again and hop onto the highway. I know this won't change how things will turn out, but I'm determined to put as many miles as possible between her and myself.

I like this girl. She deserves better.

She deserves someone whole to hold her without breaking into so many pieces—and that'll never be me.

RICK
"THE REAPER"

No. We're not leaving. Not today anyway. I steer the wheel and turn the car around, heading back to town. She's hurt me. She's insulted me. She makes me feel like an idiot.

Leaving isn't how this ends.

I will fix this.

I will right the wrongs.

For all of us, whether they want it or not.

She's mine.

She will stay.

JAMES
"THE PROTECTOR"

I snatch the wheel and take back control. My heart pounds against my chest. No. I can't let Rick go back. I love her—not just the *watch-her-from-afar* sort of way. I'm willing to do what the others can't. I'm willing to—I steer the wheel and turn the car around, facing the oncoming traffic. My eyes land on a truck, heading my way.

He doesn't get to touch her. Not while I'm in control.

I kick the gas.

Daisy. My perfect girl. This, I'll do for you.

I wake up to myself passing Sterling's city limit. The sky has already darkened. I'm in a new shirt. Still alive. Still warm.

I pull over and stop the engine. I check myself from head to toe, then step out to inspect the truck.

There isn't a dent. Not even a scratch. The only thing noticeable is the lower end of the truck, coated in dust—like I've driven through the desert or something. But as far as I can tell, nothing's happened.

I'm clean. Almost a little too clean.

I stand on the side of the road, feeling like I've missed something.

Is Daisy still okay?

My heart lurches.

No—

He's gone back to her. He wouldn't let it end like that.

No, no, no... I need to find her. I need to see for myself. She could still be alive. She could be.

I climb back into the truck and restart the engine. I pull onto the road and kick the gas.

Ten minutes later, I walk into the diner and catch the first waitress I see.

"Is Daisy here?" I ask, hoping she'll tell me my girl's been here the whole time.

She should be here. Her shift doesn't end until later tonight.

"No. She didn't come to work today," the waitress says without looking at me.

"Do you know why?"

"No. Sorry."

"Did she call the diner?"

"I don't... sorry."

The waitress hurries away, called to another customer, and I'm left standing in the Denny's she works at, not sure what to think anymore.

A horrid, sickening feeling wraps its arms around me.

I can't breathe.

Did he...?

No. I refuse to believe it.

DEAN

"MAINTENANCE"

I take the helm from James and get back in the car, trying her number. It goes straight to voicemail. I frown and call her house instead.

The call is picked up after a moment. I recognize her grandma Nina's voice and let out a small sigh of relief.

"Hello?"

"Hello," I say. "I'm a friend of Daisy's. She didn't come to work today. I just wanted to check if she's okay."

"She didn't come to work?" Nina asks, surprised.

"No," I say.

"Oh," Nina murmurs. "Did you check the diner?"

"I was there earlier."

"Well, I haven't seen her since yesterday," she says. "I went to the market this morning and had my eyes checked this afternoon."

"Do you know where she might be?"

"Sorry, dear," she says. "Have you tried her cell?"

"I have."

"That's very strange indeed. Very strange." She pauses. "Daisy never misses a day of work. She's very punctual... Are you sure she's not at the diner?"

I sigh. I'm pretty sure.

I thank her and hang up, then start the truck. I decide to check the places she likes first, then move on to other establishments. If she's in one of them, I'll find her. If she's not, I'll keep looking. I give myself a deadline. Ten o'clock. If I can't find her by then, I'll return to her house and wait. If she doesn't show up by morning... I suppose I'll have my answer.

At ten, my hands tighten on the wheel, unable to carry out my own directive. I know what I'm supposed to do, but I just can't. Up until now, I haven't allowed myself to feel anything. My job is to find her. The job isn't finished—but I have a good idea where she might be.

My truck is dirty. My hands are way too clean. She's not at work. Not in any of the places she frequents.

I turn the truck and head to the pier, hollow.

There's a hole in my chest every time I think of her. Our last exchange. The things I wanted to say and never got around to.

I need something louder, bigger—something massive enough to fill the space. She's not mine to care about. I don't even like her. I just can't stop thinking about her.

It's like a sickness.

I park my truck and walk the length of the pier as it

stretches into the ocean. White noise wraps me in, but still, I can't feel my face or my legs. Emptiness is all I feel—until I realize someone is singing at the end of the pier.

Disappointed, I shake my head, ready to leave—then the voice catches, sounding a little like hers.

I pause. My heart races.

For a moment, I listen to the woman sing, letting myself pretend it's her. I think I've been thinking about her too much. Perhaps I've gone crazy... but the more I listen, the more it sounds like her.

My legs start moving again, heading toward the voice. They freeze the moment I can see clearly.

"Daisy!" I call, my voice trembling.

She turns, startled.

"Rick?"

RICK

"THE REAPER"

"Daisy," I whisper her name, bitter and painful. There she is. Alive. Drunk. A little lost and a little broken. Sitting on the rail with a bottle of wine in her hand, wobbling.

"Rick... what are you doing here?" Her voice is unsteady.

I walk toward her and pull her into a kiss, holding her steady. No. She doesn't get to ask me that. Not while she's doing this to herself.

"I thought I made myself clear," I say, my chest still aching.

"What?" She seems lost. Her fingers clutch at my chest.

"This."

I groan and grab a handful of her hair, pulling it to the side to expose the scar. She gasps, pressing her hand to my chest. Her body tenses.

I force her closer and trail my mouth to the bite mark behind her ear—sucking it, kissing it, biting it. I feel myself getting shamefully hard, even though the mere thought of someone else once doing this to her makes me sick. So I break skin, making it mine.

"I don't fucking care," I whisper harshly, my fist tightening in her hair. "You're mine. You get that?"

"But I thought you hated me."

"No. Shut it."

I take her mouth, cutting her words. My gaze pins her. My teeth drag over her lower lip until there's iron on my tongue.

"From now on, no one gets to do fucked-up shit to you except me." I grab the wine bottle from her hand and throw it into the ocean. "If a guy so much as looks at you a second longer, I'll break his teeth and cut off his fingers. Then I'll put a knife into his pathetic little heart and bury him in the desert."

She gasps, pulling her legs together.

I part them, forcing her to meet my eyes.

"With the rest."

She freezes.

"Say you understand."

I squeeze her chin and tip her face skyward, driving her back over the rail. My hand bites into her waist, anchoring her there. She lets out a small scream and grabs onto me.

"Say you understand." I raise my voice.

Her fingers tighten. Her pupils dilate.

"I understand," she murmurs, breathless.

"Good."

I haul her back against my chest.

"Don't do fucked-up shit like this again."

She gives a small nod. Her arms come around me, still rattled by what I just did. Then, as if it hits her all at once, she pulls me in and kisses me, deeply and desperately.

It surprises me that she doesn't use her teeth this time —like she's suddenly learned how to kiss like a normal person. Just tongue and lips and feeling. Wet. Soft. Her hand guides mine between her legs again.

I want to give in. I want to fuck her right here on this rail. I fucking do. But I can't get into it. I keep seeing her in the water. The thought of how long it took me to find her twists something sharp in my chest. If I'd arrived an hour later, would she still be here? Is she really that stupid?

I've threatened her. I've fixed the mark. But that fear in my gut—it's still there.

XAXE

"THE ANNIHILATOR"

I only meet with people under extreme circumstances. Either they know they're about to die, or they don't. The end result never changes.

Except Rick, none of the others know I exist. They think Rick and I are one, but the truth is always worse.

For months, I've heard about this girl from the people I meet. I've been waiting for this day, but our appointment has been postponed so many times that I began to think it would never happen.

I lean against the rail, studying her. I've given a lot of thought to how we'd meet. Her sitting on a rail, quietly contemplating her own demise, isn't what I'd expect. And as far as I can tell, being pulled back wasn't part of her plan for the night.

This is a first.

I let out a sigh and bring my legs over the rail to sit beside her. From my pocket, I take out a flask and hand it to her. She chugs it, then throws it into the ocean. I watch it disappear, not sure whether I should tell her the flask she just tossed away like garbage belonged to my grandfather.

"How do I know you're not just saying all of this?" she breaks the silence at last. "You say the perfect thing, Rick. You do the perfect thing—the most romantic thing anyone has ever done for me. And then you undo it."

She looks at me, something broken in her eyes.

"I'm confused..." she mutters. "Last night, you covered me in marks. This morning, you covered them up. You said you wanted me to stay yours forever. Then you took me to a pharmacy, fucked me raw in a bathroom, and made me take the pills. And now you're back, saying you forgive me for the scars Dylan put on me, but you don't even look at me the same. And still, you're here. With me. At the pier."

"You're dating a crazy person," I sigh. "That's what it is."

I mean it.

"Every part of me wants you just for me. One part is terrified I've already hurt you. Another is convinced that I have. And there's a part that exists only to make sure nothing I do ever hurts you—only to fail and bring me right back here."

She looks up at me, her eyes misty.

"That's..."

"Psychotic," I murmur. "Emotional. Unstable. Possessive. Jealous. Delusional."

"Yeah." She laughs drily. "That sounds like you."

I wait for her to finish laughing.

"Did I put you here?" My voice softens. "Was I the reason?"

"Don't kid yourself." She flashes a look at me and shakes her head. "We barely know each other." But the way she lowers her head, looking a little broken and lost, tells me otherwise. So I keep staring at her until she's ready to tell me the truth.

"I feel... really broken after you left," she says, unable to look at me. "It's not you. It's me. We had a one-night stand. I know how it works, but I gave myself all those marks to have something to look at. I just never thought about how it would feel when you left."

I frown.

"Do you know what the worst part is?"

"It's not the first time you've felt this way," I whisper.

She looks up at me, a little shocked. Then, slowly, she nods.

"Yeah."

"I figured." I sigh, wrapping an arm around her and pulling her closer.

That's why I did what I did.

"There's something really broken in me, Rick," she says quietly. "Like I need someone to hold me together. I'm always in pieces. Shattered. Bloody. I try to glue myself back together—showing up to work, dating, paying taxes, smiling. But no matter what I do, I'll never be whole, and everyone knows. They see me. And they stay away."

I reach out to take her hand, but end up squeezing it instead.

"Do you know that earlier today, a part of me tried to run into traffic so I wouldn't come back here and ruin your life?"

She freezes.

"I'm a little broken myself, Daisy," I sigh. "And this thing we have—it's unhealthy."

"No."

"If you want out," I say quietly, "I'll let you out."

No harm.

She shakes her head hard and reaches into her pocket. She pulls out the Plan B pills and throws them into the ocean. Then she glares at me, her lips trembling, unable to speak.

"My offer stands if you want it one day."

"Fuck one day," she says stubbornly, taking my arm hostage. As if that isn't enough, she takes my hand and pulls it to her mouth, biting down hard—holding on until I promise not to leave.

"Okay," I whisper. "No way out."

Only then does she let go.

I tip her chin up and press a kiss to her lips.

She settles back against my shoulder. After a while, her breathing evens out, soft snoring slipping free as she wears herself out.

I brush my face against the top of her head, my mind

drifting back to everything I've done since the day Rick spotted her in that diner.

"I killed Dylan today, Daisy," I whisper, knowing she can't hear me. "That was the last of your shitty ex-boyfriends."

I press a kiss to her hair and close my eyes.

"It was always you or them. Rick chose you every time. Now, I get it. I choose you too."

She's Daisy.

And I'm me.

I won't hesitate to burn the world down. I don't even need a reason.

But her, I refuse.

We can stay on the rail a little longer.

THE END UNTIL IT'S NOT

Afterword

If you enjoyed this book, don't forget to leave me a review so others can find it too :)

I don't usually write sequels unless there's a good reason. Wanna be my reason? Nominate this book for a sequel here: https://www.thepunkhead.com/nominate-a-sequel

I'll be back soon!

ALSO BY KATRINA YANG

His Winter Baby
(A Dark Captive Romantic Thriller)

On her way home for the holidays, Casey's car breaks down in the mountains.

With a storm closing in, she has no other choice but to take a ride from a stranger...

In a cabin deep in the wilderness where no one can hear her scream, she becomes his new obsession until spring comes.

Amazon | Website

Pretty Girl
(A Spicy Thriller)

He's the masked host.

She's the girl in a blindfold in front of a camera.

The world is watching. There's no private view.

Only he is allowed to touch her.

And he breaks her softly, brutally, lovingly—

until wanting him feels inevitable.

Amazon | Website

Night Clerk
(A Motel 808 Thriller)

One room. One motel. A killing game. A new hire.

Motel 808 has a dark past no one talks about. There's a reason guests stay on the ground floor. Curiosity has a cost—enter at your own risk.

Amazon | Website